Rip Squeak and His Friends

an introduction to
The Roaring Adventures of Rip Squeak

Illustrations by Leonard Filgate
Story by Susan Yost-Filgate

Rip Squeak, Inc.

For further information regarding Rip Squeak, including licensing and the purchase of fine art originals and reproductions, please contact:

Beda Schmidthues
Rip Squeak, Inc.
2603 Broad Street
San Luis Obispo, CA 93401

Telephone: (805) 594-0184
Facsimile: (805) 543-5782

URL: http://www.RipSqueak.com
e-mail: info@RipSqueak.com

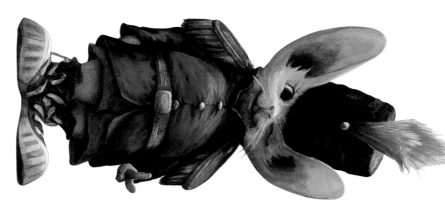

Filgate™

Second Edition, Second Printing

© 1999-2001 Leonard Filgate and Susan Yost-Filgate

RIP SQUEAK™, FILGATE™, and FILGATE & Design™
are trademarks of Leonard Filgate

Published by Rip Squeak, Inc, Carmel-by-the-Sea, California USA
in cooperation with Baumhaus Medien AG, Frankfurt am Main, Germany

ISBN: 0-9 9672422-C-7

Distribution in Germany, Austria and Switzerland by Baumhaus Medien AG, Seelenberger Straße 4, D-60489 Frankfurt/Main
Order number: ISBN 3-909484-55-7

Printed in Italy by Societa Editoriale Grafiche AZ

500 copies of the First edition are included in a limited special edition, encased in a cloth-covered box with
a copy of an art print personally signed and numbered by the artist Leonard Filgate.

For Jessica, Julia, and Anna
and
for the child in each of us.

This is a story about Rip Squeak and his little sister Jesse and their strange friendships with Abbey, an abandoned kitten, and a frog named Euripides. Rip and Jesse live inside the walls of a summer cottage which is seldom inhabited by humans. Their lives take on a whole new direction when they meet Abbey, who prefers to befriend creatures like mice and frogs and birds rather than other cats. Abbey introduces Rip and Jesse to her friend, Euripides, a very entertaining actor and storyteller who lives and breathes the theater.

Through Rip's own words, this book introduces the story of the meeting of these creatures and the friendships that develop, setting the stage for the adventures yet to come. The book also introduces the most wonderful and whimsical work of Artist, Leonard Filgate. His memorable images bring Rip Squeak and his friends to life.

An Introduction

Leonard Filgate was introduced to me in 1997 while I was the director of Joie de Vivre Gallery in Carmel, California. The gallery's concept was to exhibit art that was playful and happy, not simply whimsical, but art that touched the emotional heart in a positive, happy, and uplifting way.

From the moment that Leonard unveiled his first painting to me, I knew that his art would impact the lives of children and adults alike. It would teach and entertain children and delight and tickle the child in adults. Before that meeting, Tom Barnes, the owner of Joie de Vivre, had said to me, "I don't want paintings that are in any way ugly or scary to children." Leonard's were neither. There was an innocence and vulnerability to the animal characters, and the paintings were little masterpieces, painted with great attention given to the drawing, expression, proportion, composition, light, color and content. I had expected to see "cute" illustrations. Instead they were beautifully painted original works.

After Leonard finished showing us the paintings came an extra bonus — I was handed a folder with a manuscript entitled *The Roaring Adventures of Rip Squeak*, written by Leonard's wife, Susan. It then occurred to me that this was more than just another artist; it was a husband/wife, artist/writer team. As I got to know Leonard and Susan, along with their daughter Jessica, I realized what a wonderful team they make.

Quickly reading through the story, while surrounded by the paintings of all the existing characters, I felt as though I had been transported into the cottage where Rip and his friends live, prey and predator harmoniously living together as unlikely friends. The story begins with Abbey, a small abandoned kitten, being found by a little mouse, Rip Squeak and his younger sister Jesse. Rip, whose fear of cats was overcome by his compassion for the sobbing kitten, befriended Abbey — and there the adventures start.

The paintings Leonard showed us that day were just a prelude to what would come. A short time later, the gallery was sent three or four paintings. We immediately hung them. It was such fun to watch people light up with smiles when they looked at the paintings. Many, after leaving the gallery, would reappear later with someone else in tow so they could share their great discovery. The first painting sold to a man from Scotland for his music room, which proved I was correct — the work appealed to adults too. The painting was of Rip's friend Euripides, a frog, standing on a piano beside a music sheet, singing.

The painting that will, to me, always most represent *The Roaring Adventures of Rip Squeak* is "Harmony". The painting is a "family" of little characters gathered around a piano — Rip dancing on the keys, Abbey playing a tune, and Euripides singing with little Jesse and Rip's parents happily enjoying the whole event. This painting symbolizes what Leonard and Susan's collaborative works are about: getting along together despite differences.

Sheri Barnes
A friend of Rip Squeak

The Lay of the Land
The Cottage and Euripides' Pond

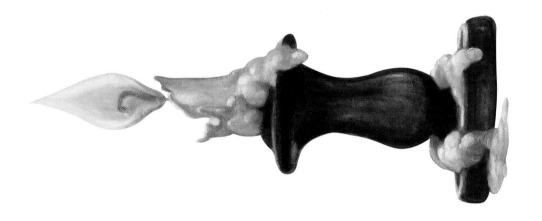

The Story

One morning the humans left our cottage, taking all their suitcases with them. The house was soooo quiet. As we tiptoed to the kitchen, my little sister Jesse whispered, "Are you sure all the cats went too?"

"Don't worry," I said, sniffing the air. "One thing I'm sure of, somebody left a cinnamon bun on that counter. I'll climb up and you get ready to catch it."

That's when we heard the sound every mouse dreads: "Me-eeeeoowwww . . ."

"Cat!" My brain screamed. Jesse and I both froze against the wall. All I could think of was my father

saying "protect your sister." My whiskers quivered and my knees knocked together. "Be brave . . . be brave," I muttered to myself. Dad had always said you have to be brave, even when you're scared. I peeked around the corner into the kitchen. What I saw was a kitten crying pitifully.

Jesse clutched my arm. "It's okay," I whispered, as I pulled away from her grasp. But I hated to see anyone so sad. Call me stupid. Call me brave. Call me realizing that I was even moving, I suddenly found myself a claw's length from the sobbing kitten.

"Rip!" Jesse squealed. "Let's run!"

I couldn't. That kitten's sobs really got to me. "Exc-c-cuse me," I stammered, "M-m-my n-name is Rip Squeak. Could I help you?"

The kitten looked at me with tearful, startled eyes. It was too late to worry that I looked like a snack to her. "I'm Abigail," she said, snuffling. "My family calls me Abbey. That is, they did before they went away without me. I'm all alone now!" She meowed woefully again. Then she took a breath and told me she'd been born in this same country cottage that was our home too. But when the Winemores went back to their house in the city, she'd somehow gotten left behind.

"It's okay," I soothed. "You've got us. That's my sister Jesse over there." I pointed to Jesse, whose eyes were huge with fright as she clutched Bunny, her favorite doll. "You're not alone, Abbey."

Jesse shrieked at that question. "Cat! Cat! Cat!" she hissed, gesturing wildly. "We're mice! Mice! Mice!"

"You mean that, Rip?"

"You bet I do. We'll help you. Are you hungry?"

"I know where there's a cinnamon bun," I said quickly. "We could share it with you." My heart was pounding. What if Abbey said she liked the taste of mice better?

"Oh, I love cinnamon buns!" Abbey exclaimed.

Suddenly Jesse was by my side. "Then you won't eat us?"

"Of course not!" Abbey looked shocked at the idea. "I would never eat my friends!"

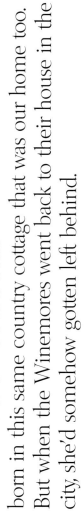

The next morning Jesse and I found Abbey in the backyard chewing on some plant leaves. They must have tasted even better to her than cinnamon buns because she flopped down and started rolling in them! When she saw us, she sat up and began carefully washing her face with her paw.

"I was just treating myself to some catnip," she said. "Would you like to try it?"

Before we could answer, she twitched her ears, quirked her whiskers, and stared at something we couldn't see, the way cats do when their imagination sends them ideas.

14

She scampered around us, gently chasing butterflies as she told us about her friend Euripides, an actor who lived by the pond. Jesse and I had never ventured as far as the pond. To us it was a wild and dangerous place.

"You'll be safe with me!" Abbey promised. "I'll even give you a ride!" She crouched down so we could climb aboard. Soon we were moving at the speed of kitten, the countryside whizzing by.

At the pond we could hear clapping and cheering. Then a frog leaped onto a lily pad before us. He had on weird, baggy shorts, a funny jacket with stiff shoulders, and a shirt with puffy sleeves and ruffles that stuck out all around his neck. He wore a sword at his side, and as he bowed to us he made a grand sweep with a hat that had a giant feather stuck in it.

"Abbey, my dear," he said in a regal voice. "How good of you to come by before you left for the city — though why you'd want to go there is beyond me. The noise! The crowds! The ridiculous prices for theater tickets!" He rolled his bulging eyes and shook his green head. "But then you are an odd cat. How like you to have mice for friends. What's next? Dogs? Birds?"

When Abbey introduced us, Jesse and I said, "Pleased to meet you, sir."

"Bah!" the frog scoffed. "Call me Eur-rribbit-ribbit-ribbit—" He frowned and tried again. "Call me Eur-ribbit-ribbit—" He cleared his throat and said, "Pardon me a moment. An actor must constantly practice the art of speaking clearly." His tongue began to flutter and his throat began to vibrate. "Frreckled frrogs frrolic frrreely," he recited over and over. "Frrreckled frrrogs frrrolic frrreely."

Finally he nodded and grinned at us. "Call me Euripides!" he demanded cheerfully. "Now then, Abbey, why so glum?"

"I'm not going to the city," she told him. "I got left behind!"

"Indeed!" Euripides blustered. "That won't do. We shall have to improvise."

"What's improvise?" all three of us asked.

"Why, it's simply making the most of an unexpected situation," he answered.

"Like having an adventure!" I piped up.

"Positively, my boy," Euripides agreed, patting my shoulder. "Well said."

It rained Saturday morning, spoiling my plans to do stuff outdoors. I didn't even feel like getting out of bed. How would Euripides handle rotten luck like this?

It sure would be cool to be like him, I thought. He seemed so smart. And, well, somebody who knows how the world works.

That reminded me I'd better check on Jesse. Unlike me, she loved playing in the rain. But she was too little to watch out for herself. She might need her big brother.

I found Bunny propped up on the windowsill in the sunroom. Jesse was on the patio in her raincoat and boots, happily twirling her umbrella as she splashed in puddles.

While I watched her I saw movement in the bushes behind her. Probably just Abbey taking cover from the storm, I thought. That's when I saw two glowing yellow eyes staring out at my sister. "Jesse!" I yelled, pounding on the window. "Behind you! Strange cat!"

But Jesse was lost in her own world. She didn't see the giant yellow tom cat slink out of the bushes, licking its fangs and drooling.

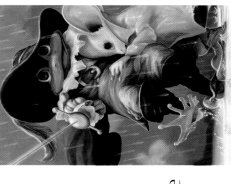

Out of nowhere Euripides dashed between my sister and the beast, dressed like a Musketeer and waving a long, shiny sword as he hopped around and yelled! That's when Jesse finally saw him too. She dropped her umbrella and took cover against Euripides.

Then Abbey appeared, her back arched ferociously. She was hissing, spitting, and screeching, trying her best to look twice her size and three times as tough as the intruder.

That's when Jesse really surprised us all. As if getting a shot of courage, she suddenly reached behind her, grabbed her umbrella, and using it like Euripides' sword, she poked the evil-eyed monster right in the nose! They were an awesome team. The totally confused enemy cat turned tail and ran.

I was so proud of my friends and my little sister I whooped in victory.

Abbey and Euripides congratulated Jesse and each other and grinned at me. Then Euripides scooped Jesse up in his long arms and brought her into the house.

"Rip!" Jesse cried, racing to me for a hug, "He almost got me, but I fought back!"

"You sure did! You won!" I held her tight, not even caring that she was cold and wet.

"We're heroes, huh?" said Jesse, looking up at me.

"All for one and one for all," Euripides declared, gallantly raising his sword.

Then Euripides added, "We've earned some tea! There's nothing like a hot cup of tea to soothe the nerves."

We sat on the kitchen counter for the rest of the morning, sipping our tea and listening to Euripides tell stories about his life as an actor. We all started to relax.

When Euripides saw we were calmed down from our scare, he stood up and bowed. "You are wonderful listeners. But I must go off to the theater."

"But it's still raining," I reminded him.

"Bah! The show must go on."

As he headed for the cat door, I called after him, "What'll we do for the rest of the day until you come back?"

"Silly boy," Euripides replied, "use your imagination!"

So we did. We played games and told ghost stories and read books. We made popcorn and made up silly jokes and laughed so hard it hurt. Then Mom and Dad asked Jesse and me to help with chores. I forlornly looked at Abbey and said, "I don't think you can fit in our rooms."

"That's okay," Abbey yawned. "I need a little catnap."

We helped clean our rooms. Making our beds turned into a pillow fight. It was fun until we realized Abbey wasn't with us. "Let's go be with Abbey," I said to Jesse.

Abbey was sitting on the piano bench in the living room of the cottage, gingerly pressing keys with her paws.

"Hey, that sounds familiar," I told her.

"The Winemore kids used to play it," she responded with a sigh. "Oh, Rip, I miss my family!"

I didn't know how to cheer her up, and that made me feel bad. "Please don't stop playing, Abbey. It's a happy sound — maybe it'll make you happy."

Abbey's playing drew Mom and Dad into the living room too. They perched on the piano, smiling and humming along.

Suddenly there was a loud thump and an annoyed grunt from the kitchen. The music stopped and we all froze, our eyes on the kitchen door. Euripides strolled in, looking like a spy in a trench coat. "You must get that cat door fixed," he said, rubbing his backside. He took off his coat to reveal an elegant tuxedo.

"Continue playing, my sweet girl," he said to Abbey. "I feel like singing, and you're a natural."

"But I don't know any other songs," Abbey protested.

"Hmmmm." Euripides stroked his silky bow tie thoughtfully. "Why, then, we'll improvise, of course." He sprang onto the piano and leaned against the sheet music on the stand. I wanted to be up there with him, so I clambered over the keys, making an awful racket. Euripides smiled at me, nodded at Mom and Dad, and winked at Jesse cuddled next to Abbey on the bench. "Just play, darling Abigail, and I'll wing it."

As Abbey began to play again, Euripides threw back his head and let out a song in a booming operatic voice. I couldn't understand the foreign words he sang, but the sound was beautiful. It made me feel so free, I danced on the keys, changing Abbey's melody in a big way. She giggled and followed along with me, and our new tune didn't sound half bad!

"Lovely harmony!" Euripides encouraged. "That's the spirit, dear friends!"

One day Abbey made a discovery. "Come with me!" she insisted, stooping down so I could climb on her back.

"But where are we going?" I asked as she zoomed out the cat door.

"To get Euripides!" was all she would say.

I clung to her soft fur, knowing she would stop abruptly. That was the kitten way. If you weren't prepared, you could go flying and land with a thump!

Abbey halted at a pile of rocks. I realized it must be Euripides' house.

"Euripides, wake up! Wake up!" she shouted.

I went to the door and knocked on it gently, the mouse way, so as not to startle him. "Euripides," I called softly, "are you awake? Abbey has something to show us!"

I could hear him snoring. What would wake him up? Then I got an idea.

"Think, Abbey!" I said. "What's that word they yell at the pond after a play? The one that makes the actors keep coming out again and again for a bow?"

Abbey squinted, thinking hard. "Bravo! That's it!" She started shouting, "Bravo, Euripides, bravo!"

"Bravo!" I echoed her, applauding, "Bravo, Euripides!" The snoring stopped.
Within a minute, Euripides opened the door, yawning and rubbing his eyes. I tried not to giggle as he stood there swaying sleepily in his striped nightshirt and silly stocking cap.

"This better be good, you two," he mumbled. "What adventure awaits us today?"

"Abbey won't tell," I replied.

Abbey just smiled and purred.

A little while later Euripides reappeared in the oddest costume I'd seen him in yet. There were big diamond shapes on his pants. There were droopy tails tipped with little bells springing from his hat and collar.

When I looked back at Abbey, she grinned and said, "Cool, huh?"

"Great galloping grasshoppers, this is beyond cool," Euripides declared. "This is — this is marvelosity to the splen-DID-i-most degree! Think of the adventures we can have in here!"

"Oh, my," Jesse breathed in wonder. She headed straight for the mountain of stuffed animals.

"I can't believe I've lived here all my life and didn't know this room existed!" I blurted gleefully. "It's like the best birthday ever! It's like Christmas!"

"Christmas! Yes! Excellent!" Euripides agreed. "We can have Christmas every day here!"

"It's perfect!" I said. "Because ever since I met Abigail and you, every day feels like Christmas."

"Merry everything and happy always!" Abbey sang out. "You guys are the best family anybody could wish for!"

"Wow, what are you today?" I asked.

"Today, my boy, I am a court jester, a harlequin," Euripides replied. "And I'm ready to go off on Abbey's adventure."

Abbey gave us a ride back to the cottage, where we found Jesse awake and eager to go with us. I pulled Jesse and Bunny on board and we headed towards the stairs. "Hold on tight!" Abbey called out. She let us off at a door that was slightly ajar. "This is it! Are you ready?"

Abbey pushed the door open wide and stood back so we could see inside. The room was full of toys!

There were horses, dolls and teddy bears of every size and kind. There were lions perched on window sills and dogs napping on chairs. There were trains and planes and sailboats all ready to glide away, while tigers, puppets, and giraffes gathered around to watch. There were books and balls and blocks, and even a little house filled with furniture just the right size for Jesse and Euripides and me.

We played for hours, until we got hungry, and then we wandered down to the kitchen for food. Afterward we followed the warm rays of sunlight shining through the sunroom windows.

Sighing contentedly, Abbey plopped down on a plump pillow for a catnap. Euripides, Jesse, and I nestled against her, and the sound of her purring lulled us to sleep.

I dreamed of toys and magic.
I dreamed of adventures yet to come.
I dreamed of the fun we'd had so far, and all the good times my best friends and I would share from now on.

The Illustrations

The kitten looked at me with tearful, startled eyes.

Soon we were moving at the speed of kitten, the countryside whizzing by.

Then a frog leaped onto a lily pad before us.

Jesse was on the patio in her raincoat and boots, happily twirling her umbrella as she splashed in puddles.

Out of nowhere Euripides dashed between my sister and the beast, dressed like a Musketeer and waving a long shiny sword as he hopped around and yelled.

We sat on the kitchen counter, sipping our tea and listening to Euripides tell stories.

"Lovely harmony!" Euripides encouraged.

Euripides threw back his head and let out a song in booming operatic voice.

I danced on the keys, changing
Abbey's melody in a big way.

I tried not to giggle as he stood there swaying sleepily in his striped nightshirt and silly stocking cap.

I'm ready to go off on Abbey's adventure.

I pulled Jesse and Bunny on board and we headed towards the stairs.

Abbey's Surprise . . . .

"Great galloping grasshoppers, this is beyond cool," Euripides declared.

"Christmas! Yes! Excellent!" Euripides agreed. "We can have Christmas every day here!"

44

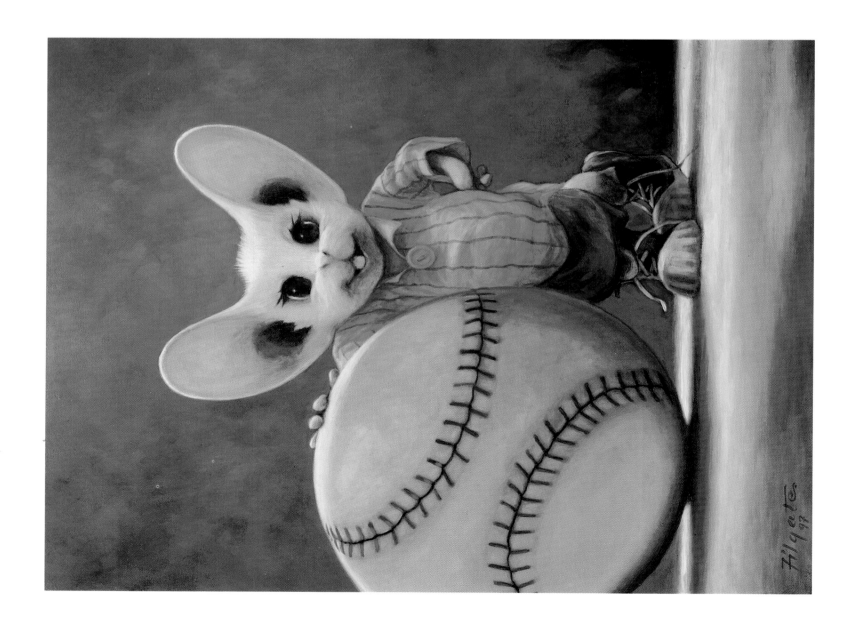

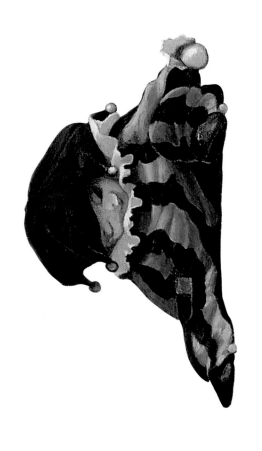

I dreamed of toys and magic. I dreamed of adventures yet to come. I dreamed of the fun we'd had so far, and all the good times my best friends and I would share from now on.

Pirate Tales

We invite you to follow
The Roaring Adventures of Rip Squeak
as Rip, Jesse, Abbey & Euripides discover
the secret of Pirate Tales . . .

and watch for more stories . . .
in the series

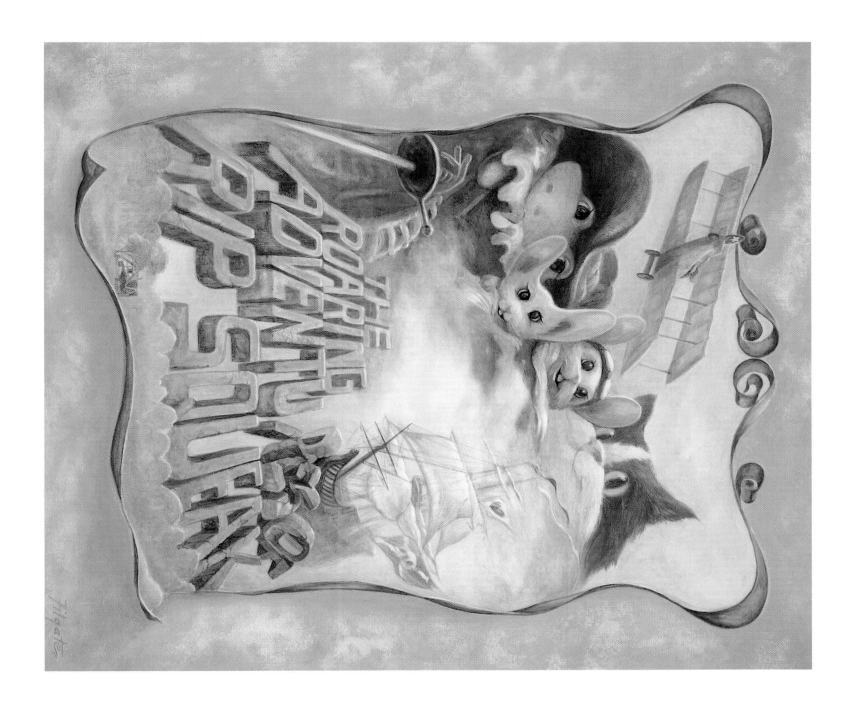

Index to the Illustrations

Title	Dimensions	Page
Harmony II	24 x 30	cover
The Cottage	18 x 24	7
Lay of the Land	24 x 36	9
The Writer	18 x 24	12
The First Meeting	12 x 16	13
Euripides' Tale	16 x 20	22
I'll Be Your Friend	24 x 36	24
Off to Meet Euripides	24 x 36	25
Meeting Euripides	24 x 36	26
Rain Dance	24 x 30	27
The Rescue	24 x 30	28
The Tea Party	24 x 30	29
Harmony I	16 x 20	30
Harmony II	24 x 30	31
Euripides' Solo	12 x 16	32
Rip's Dance	12 x 16	33
Good Morning	24 x 36	34
The Jester's Gesture	16 x 20	35
Getting a Lift	24 x 30	36
Abbey's Surprise	16 x 20	38

Leonard Filgate
The Illustrator

Leonard is an artist of remarkable ability. His art training came from life experiences, his own studies of the great masters, and his diligence. His innate ability to bring canvas to life is pure magic, as is witnessed in the wonderful illustrations in this book.

As a child, Leonard would roam the streets of San Francisco on bicycle, spending hours in art museums and exploring Golden Gate Park observing all that his eyes could absorb. He later spent five years traveling throughout Southeast Asia, the South Pacific, and the Mediterranean while serving in the United States Merchant Marine. Leonard has been refining his art for over thirty years. His work has included everything from marine painting for the United States Navy, to theatrical backdrops, to reproductions of Japanese screens, to the incredible whimsical works on these pages.

The art he is creating now gives him the greatest satisfaction. It may have been sparked by the childhood of his daughter, but it has continued because of his own love for the imaginary, happy world he is painting. It has long been Leonard's philosophy that art imitate the best in life, whether it be from reality or from deep within our imagination. Art should be an oasis in a chaotic world, an elixer that will bring a smile to our soul.

Susan Yost-Filgate
The Writer

Susan has been writing stories and poetry since high school. Her interest in work for children was influenced by both her experiences in teaching and the birth of her daughter Jessica in 1984. She and her husband Leonard, embarked on this project, *The Roaring Adventures of Rip Squeak* in 1997. Susan wrote this story as a showcase for her husband, Leonard's incredible talents. Although it is their first published book, it is one of many creative projects which they have developed together since joining forces in 1977. It will not be their last, as Susan has a file full of ideas which have yet to be developed.

Originally from Pennsylvania, Susan headed to San Francisco, California after college, in route to Ibiza, Spain (she obviously missed a turn somewhere . . .). She fell in love with the city and soon after fell in love with Leonard. After nearly 22 years of city dwelling, Susan, Leonard and Jessica left the big city for a quieter life in a small town in California.

Susan holds a bachelor's degree in art education from The Pennsylvania State University. She has taught art, worked as a graphic designer, and as a paralegal. Her time is now absorbed in being a parent and in this and other related projects.

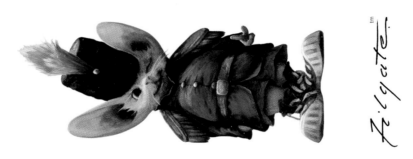

The Filgates wish to thank Beda and Helga Schmidthues for their
everlasting friendship and faith in this project, from the beginning.

Additional thanks go to John Jepson, Connie Fulton, Sandy Phillips,
Sheri Barnes, Frank Dobronte, Tom Barnes, Dick and Lana Vento

and

everyone else who has been a part of this project
by bringing Rip Squeak and his friends into their homes and hearts.
Without each of you, Rip would have remained
just another wonderful idea on a shelf.

Additional credits to:

First Impressions of Carmel Valley, California for the greeting card design entitled "Christmas Antics", a computer-generated compilation created from artwork by Leonard Filgate.

Martha Casanave of Monterey, California for black and white photographs of the illustrator and writer.